Chloe

The Usborne Book of Fairy Tales

Retold by Heather Amery
Illustrated by Stephen Cartwright
Language consultant: Betty Root
Series editor: Jenny Tyler

First published in 2004 by Usborne Publishing Ltd, 83-85 Saffron Hill, London EC1N 8RT, England. www.usborne.com
 UE. This edition first published in America in 2005. Printed in China.

Contents

There's a little yellow duck to find on every page.

Cinderella

Remember there is a little yellow duck to find on every page.

That's Cinderella looking out of the window.

She lives with her Stepmother and two ugly Stepsisters.

They are always really horrible to her.

They make her work all day.

She cleans the house and cooks the meals. She wears old clothes and sleeps in a cold, creepy room.

They are all asked to a Grand Ball at the palace.

The two Stepsisters are so excited. "We must have new dresses, and look our very best," they scream.

The great day comes.

The Stepsisters get ready for the Grand Ball. "May I come?" asks Cinderella. "NO, NO, NO," they shout.

Cinderella sits down and cries.

Suddenly she sees her Fairy Godmother. "Do as I tell you and you shall go to the Ball," says Fairy Godmother.

“Bring me these things.”

Cinderella brings Fairy Godmother a pumpkin, six white mice, a brown rat in a cage, and six green lizards.

Fairy Godmother waves her magic wand.

In a flash, the pumpkin is a coach, the mice are horses, the rat a coachman and the lizards are footmen.

Then Cinderella has a lovely dress and shoes.

"Go to the Ball," says Fairy Godmother. "But you must leave before the clock strikes midnight."

Cinderella goes to the palace.

The Prince meets her at the door. Everyone thinks she's a Princess. She has a lovely evening dancing with the Prince.

Then the clock strikes twelve.

"It's midnight. I must go," cries Cinderella. She runs down the palace stairs so fast one of her shoes falls off.

She runs all the way home.

She sits in the kitchen in her old clothes. Then the Stepsisters come home. They tell Cinderella about the Princess.

Next day, the Prince is very unhappy.

He wants to find the Princess. He has found her shoe.

"I'll marry the girl who can wear this shoe," he says.

The Stepsisters try on the shoe.

They push and pull. They scream and cry. The shoe is much too small for their big, ugly feet.

"May I try?" says Cinderella.

Of course, the shoe fits perfectly. Suddenly Fairy Godmother appears and changes her clothes into a lovely dress.

"I have found you," says the Prince.

"Will you marry me?" "Yes, please," Cinderella says.
They live in the palace, and are always very happy.

Sleeping Beauty

Remember there is a little yellow duck to find on every page. 

This is a good, kind King and his Queen.

After many years, the Queen has a baby girl. The King and Queen are delighted, and love the little Princess.

The baby Princess is christened.

Six good fairies come to the feast at the palace. The King forgets to invite the seventh fairy, who is nasty and wicked.

Five good fairies make good wishes for the baby.

The sixth good fairy is just about to make her wish. Then, suddenly, the wicked fairy appears, looking very angry.

"She'll prick her finger on a spinning wheel."

"Then she'll die," she says. "No," says the good fairy. "My wish is she won't die, but will sleep for a hundred years."

The Queen cries and the King shouts.

"All spinning wheels in my kingdom must be burned," he orders. "Then the Princess can't prick her finger on one."

When she grows up the Princess has a Grand Ball.

It's her seventeenth birthday. The six good fairies come to the palace. Everyone has forgotten the wicked fairy.

The next day, the Princess finds a little staircase.

She has never seen it before. In a room at the top is an old woman, with a spinning wheel. It's the wicked fairy in disguise.

"What are you doing?" asks the Princess.

"I'm spinning. Come, I'll show you," says the old woman. The Princess puts out her hand and pricks her finger.

At once, she falls fast asleep.

Everyone else in the palace goes to sleep too. The six good fairies carry the Princess to her bed. The wicked fairy disappears.

Nothing moves in the palace for a hundred years.

Outside, a thick forest grows up around it. Only the roof shows above the tree tops. The good fairies watch over the palace.

Then a young Prince walks near the palace.

He sees the roof and asks an old man about it.

"A Princess sleeps in there," he says, "but there's no way in."

The Prince walks to the palace.

The trees move apart and let him through. He runs up the steps and in through the open door. It is very quiet.

The Prince finds the Princess asleep.

She is so beautiful, he kisses her very gently. She opens her eyes and smiles. "You've come at last," she says.

Everyone in the palace wakes up.

"I'm hungry," says the King. "Tonight we'll have a great feast," and he thanks the Prince for saving them.

The Prince asks if he may marry the Princess.

"Of course," says the King. "Yes, please," says the Princess. Soon there's a grand wedding, and they're always happy.

Little Red Riding Hood

Remember there is a little yellow duck to find on every page.

This is Little Red Riding Hood and her mother.

They live near a big, dark forest. Her name comes from a bright red cloak with a hood that her Granny made her.

"Please take this food to your Granny."

"She's unwell in bed," says her mother. "Go through the forest but don't talk to any strangers you meet on the way."

Little Red Riding Hood waves goodbye.

She walks into the forest with her basket. She doesn't see the Big Black Wolf watching her from behind a tree.

Suddenly the Wolf is on the path.

"Where are you going?" he asks. "I'm taking this food to my Granny," says Red Riding Hood, feeling very scared.

The Wolf smiles a horrible smile.

"Take your Granny some flowers," he says. Red Riding Hood is even more scared. "Yes, Mr. Wolf," she says.

Red Riding Hood stops to pick some flowers.

The Wolf smiles again showing his sharp teeth. Then he runs away through the forest. He is very, very hungry.

The Wolf reaches Granny's cottage.

Granny is sitting up in bed. The Wolf pushes open the door and runs in. He gobbles up Granny in one gulp.

He climbs into Granny's bed.

He puts on her night cap and glasses. He pulls up the quilt and waits for Red Riding Hood to come.

Red Riding Hood knocks on Granny's door.

"It's me, Granny," she says. "Come in, my dear," calls the Wolf in a squeaky voice. "I'm in my bedroom."

"Hello, Granny," says Red Riding Hood.

Then she stares. "What big eyes you've got," she says.

"All the better to see you with," squeaks the Wolf.

"What big ears you've got," says Red Riding Hood.

"All the better to hear you with," squeaks the Wolf.

Red Riding Hood drops her flowers. She is very scared indeed.

"What big teeth you've got," she says.

"All the better to eat you with." Red Riding Hood screams but the Wolf gobbles her up. Then he gets back into bed.

A woodsman hears the scream.

He runs as fast as he can to the cottage. He goes in the door and straight into Granny's bedroom.

He sees the Wolf and kills it.

Inside the Wolf are Red Riding Hood and her Granny.

They are alive and very happy to be rescued.

"Thank you for saving us," says Granny.

"The Wolf can never scare anyone again." And they all sit down at the table to have cake and coffee.

Three Little Pigs

Remember there is a little yellow duck to find on every page.

A Mother Pig has three baby pigs.

One day she says, "You've grown too big for my little house. It's time you had houses of your own."

The three little Pigs trot down the road.

"Goodbye," calls Mother Pig. "Build your houses and never open the door to the Big Bad Wolf. He'll eat you."

The first little Pig meets a man.

He has a big bundle of straw. "Please give me some straw," says the little Pig. The man gives him lots of straw.

The little Pig builds his house.

He is very proud of it. It has two doors, two windows and a fine roof. "I'll be safe and snug inside," he says.

The second little Pig meets a man.

He has a big load of sticks. "Please give me some sticks," says the little Pig. The man gives him lots of big sticks.

The little Pig builds his house.

It has strong walls, two doors, two windows and a chimney.

"I'll be safe and snug inside," he says.

The third little Pig meets a man.

He has a load of bricks. "Please give me some bricks," says the little Pig. The man gives him all he needs for his house.

The little Pig builds his house.

It has thick walls, two doors, two windows and a chimney.

"I'm not afraid of the Big Bad Wolf," he says.

The Wolf comes to the straw house.

"Little Pig, let me in," he says. "No, Mr. Wolf," says the Pig. The Wolf huffs and puffs, and blows the house down.

The little Pig runs to the stick house.

Soon the Wolf comes to the door. "Little Pigs, let me in," he says. "No, no, we won't, Mr. Wolf," say the two little Pigs.

The Wolf huffs and puffs, and blows the house down.

The two little Pigs run to the brick house. Soon the Wolf comes to the door. "Little Pigs, let me in," he says.

"No, no, no, we won't," say the Pigs.

The Wolf huffs and puffs. He puffs and huffs but he can't blow the house down. He looks around for a way in.

The Wolf jumps onto the roof.

He looks down the chimney. The three little Pigs put a big pot of water on the stove. "We're ready now," says one.

The Wolf slides down the chimney.

He falls into the big pot of water. One little Pig puts on the lid. "That's the end of the Big Bad Wolf," he says.

"Now we'll have supper."

"You can stay in my house," says one little Pig, "and the Big Bad Wolf can never, ever frighten us again."

The Story of Rumpelstiltskin

Remember there is a little yellow duck to find on every page.

This poor miller has a very clever daughter.

He boasts about her. "Sire, my daughter is so clever that she can even spin straw into gold," he tells the King.

The King takes the daughter to his palace.

He shows her a room with some straw and a spinning wheel.

"Spin it into gold by morning, or you'll die," he says.

The daughter sits down and cries.

She can't spin straw into gold. Then a little man comes in.

"What will you give me if I spin it for you?" he asks.

"I'll give you my necklace," she says.

The little man spins away all night. By morning, he has spun all the straw into gold thread. Then he disappears.

The King is very pleased with the gold.

He shows the daughter another room with more straw.

"Spin that into gold by morning, or you'll die," he says.

Soon the little man comes in.

"What will you give me if I spin this bigger pile of straw into gold for you?" he asks. "My ring," says the daughter.

In the morning the King comes in.

The little man has spun all the straw into gold. The King is very pleased. But he's greedy and wants more gold.

He takes the daughter to a bigger room.

There's a bigger pile of straw. "Spin it all by morning, or you'll die," he says. Soon the little man comes in.

"What will you give me now?" he asks.

"I've nothing left," says the daughter. "Promise to give me your first baby when you're Queen," says the little man.

In the morning, the King is delighted.

"Marry me, and we'll always be rich," he says. Soon there's a royal wedding and the daughter is the Queen.

The Queen is very happy when her first baby is born.

Then the little man comes. "If you can't guess my name in three days, I'll take your baby away," he says.

The Queen thinks of names all day and all night.

When the little man comes the next day, she says, "Is it Tom, John or Henry?" The little man says, "No, you're wrong."

The little man comes again the next day.

"Is it Bandylegs, Crooksy or Boggles?" asks the Queen. "No. One more try and I'll take the baby," says the little man.

The next day, a messenger comes to the Queen.

"I saw a little man in the woods. He was singing, 'My name is Rumpelstiltskin'," he says. "Thank you," says the Queen.

"Your name is Rumpelstiltskin," says the Queen.

The little man is very angry. He stamps the floor so hard, his foot goes through the floor. Then he disappears forever.

Goldilocks and The Three Bears

Remember there is a little yellow duck to find on every page.

The Three Bears live in a forest.

There's great big Father Bear, there's middle-sized Mother Bear, and there's tiny wee Baby Bear.

Mother Bear fills three bowls with porridge.

But it's too hot to eat. "We'll go for a walk while it cools," says Father Bear. And they go out of the cottage.

Along comes a naughty girl called Goldilocks.

She peers through the cottage window. She sees there's no one at home. She opens the door and looks in.

She sees the bowls of porridge.

She tries them all. "That one's too hot," she says. "That one's too cold. This one is just right," and she eats it all up.

Goldilocks feels sleepy.

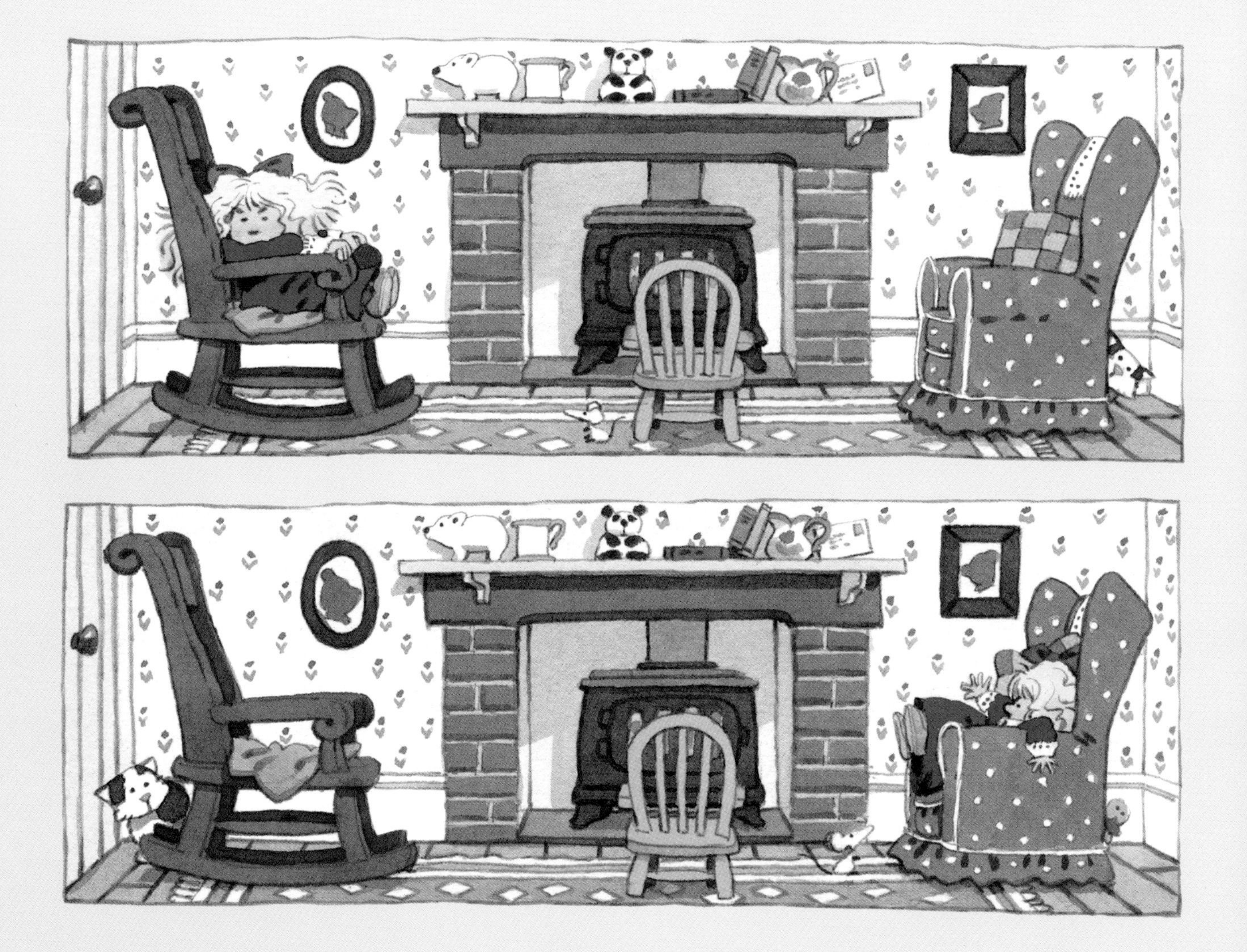

She sits on Father Bear's chair. "That's too hard," she says.

"That's too soft," she says, trying Mother Bear's chair.

She sits on Baby Bear's chair.

"This is just right," she says, and goes to sleep. There's a crack. The chair breaks and she falls on the floor.

Goldilocks goes into the bedroom.

She lies on Father Bear's bed. "That's too high," she says. She tries Mother Bear's bed. "That's too low," she says.

She lies on Baby Bear's bed.

"This is just right," she says. Soon she is fast asleep. She doesn't hear the Three Bears come into the cottage.

The Bears want their breakfast.

Father Bear says, "Who's been eating my porridge?" Mother Bear says, "Who's been eating my porridge?"

Baby Bear looks at his bowl.

"Who's been eating my porridge? And they've eaten it all up," he says. And he starts to cry big tears.

"Someone's been in here," says Father Bear.

He looks around the room. Then he looks at his chair. "Who's been sitting in my chair?" he says.

Mother Bear looks at her chair.

"Who's been sitting in my chair?" she says. "Who's been sitting in my chair, and broken it?" says Baby Bear.

The Three Bears go into the bedroom.

"Who's been sleeping in my bed?" says Father Bear.

"Who's been sleeping in my bed?" says Mother Bear.

Baby Bear looks at his bed.

"Who's been sleeping in my bed?" he says, "And, look, she's still in it." Goldilocks wakes up, very scared.

Goldilocks jumps out of bed.

She jumps out of the window and runs home to her mother.

The Three Bears never, ever see her again.